Pet Tales!

Koko the Cat

Caitie McAneney

illustrated by
Aurora Aguilera

PowerKiDS press.

New York

Published in 2018 by The Rosen Publishing Group, Inc.
29 East 21st Street, New York, NY 10010

First Edition

Managing Editor: Nathalie Beullens-Maoui
Editor, English: Elizabeth Krajnik
Book Design: Raúl Rodriguez
Illustrator: Aurora Aguilera

Cataloging-in-Publication Data

Names: McAneney, Caitie.
Title: Koko the cat / Caitie McAneney.
Description: New York : PowerKids Press, 2018. | Series: Pet tales! | Includes index.
Identifiers: ISBN 9781508156758 (pbk.) | ISBN 9781508157328 (library bound) | ISBN 9781538320334 (6 pack)
Subjects: LCSH: Cats–Juvenile fiction.
Classification: LCC PZ7.M367 Kok 2018 | DDC [E]–dc23

Manufactured in the United States of America

CPSIA Compliance Information: Batch #BS17PK: For further information contact Rosen Publishing, New York, New York at 1-800-237-9932

Contents

I am Koko the cat! I love to play.
Sometimes I get into trouble.

My best friend's name is Kayla.

She plays with me and pets my head.

I like to take naps in the sun.

Kayla thinks I sleep all day.

Kayla leaves for school.

I find my toy box. I have lots of toys!

My favorite toy is a stuffed mouse.

I throw the
mouse up
into the air.

13

I can jump very high.

I jump on tables and shelves.

I love to scratch
my post.

I can climb to
the top.

18

I like to look out
the window. I see a
squirrel and birds
outside.

19

Kayla is home!

She pours me a bowl of food.

She asks if I have been sleeping all day.

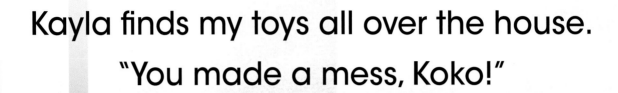

Kayla finds my toys all over the house.
"You made a mess, Koko!"

22

23

Words to Know

mouse

squirrel

toy box

Index